WORKING TOGETHER

ENCOURAGING OTHERS

BY ABBY COLICH

BLUE OWL
BOOKS

TIPS FOR CAREGIVERS

Social and emotional learning (SEL) helps children manage emotions, learn how to feel empathy, create and achieve goals, and make good decisions. Strong lessons and support in SEL will help children establish positive habits in communication, cooperation, and decision-making. By incorporating SEL in early reading, children will learn the importance of respect and encouragement when working with others.

BEFORE READING

Talk to the reader about the importance of working together and participating in group work.

Discuss: Think of a time you worked in a group. How did you communicate with the people you worked with?

AFTER READING

Talk about the importance of encouraging others and how it can positively affect group work.

Discuss: Why is it important to encourage others? What are some things you can say to encourage others?

SEL GOAL

Children may have a difficult time understanding the impact their words have, especially in a group setting in which everyone shares a common goal. Challenge readers to think about the words they use. Ask them to come up with and practice ways they can encourage, motivate, and inspire others in a group or team setting with their words.

TABLE OF CONTENTS

CHAPTER 1
Finding Strengths in Others 4

CHAPTER 2
Being a Great Teammate 8

CHAPTER 3
Helping Others 14

GOALS AND TOOLS
Grow with Goals 22
Writing Reflection 22
Glossary 23
To Learn More 23
Index 24

CHAPTER 1

FINDING STRENGTHS IN OTHERS

Working with others can be hard. It can be **rewarding**, too. You learn and grow when you work with others. It prepares you to work with others throughout your life.

As you begin working, get to know the members of your group or team. Ask what parts of the project each person is good at or wants to work on. Zion likes to paint. Mara tells Zion, "You're a good artist. I think you'll come up with some creative ideas."

All members of a group or team should **encourage** one another. Why? It builds others up. They will feel more **confident**. And you'll feel good for being **positive**.

SUPPORT EACH OTHER

Some people lack confidence in their **abilities**. Encourage them to try anyway. Say, "We know you can do it! We **support** you."

CHAPTER 1   7

CHAPTER 2

BEING A GREAT TEAMMATE

Every person on a team can help **motivate** others to get the project started and do their best. Try saying, "I'm excited to work with all of you. I think this is going to turn out great."

As you're working, let others know they are doing a good job. **Compliment** their hard work and what they do well. You could say, "I really like what you wrote!"

Sometimes, you will need to give **constructive feedback**. This means letting people know how they can improve something without hurting their feelings. If you have to do this, always start by saying something positive.

Dev and Jamal are making a book. Jamal reads what Dev wrote. He says, "I like the beginning! I think it might help to change how it ends. Can I share my ideas with you?"

CHAPTER 2

Make sure everyone feels included. Don't leave anyone out of conversations or decisions about your project.

WORDS MATTER

Never use hurtful words about the work anyone in your group has done. Even if you don't like someone's work or idea, don't put it down.

CHAPTER 2   13

CHAPTER 3

HELPING OTHERS

Some people struggle working in a group. You can help encourage them. Start by asking what's wrong. Be **patient**. Listen to what they say.

Someone may think they are doing a poor job when they're not. You can **reassure** that person. Say, "Don't be so hard on yourself. We are doing great because you are part of our group."

CHAPTER 3   15

Nico doesn't think he can finish his part of a group science fair project. Ray shows **empathy**. He tells him about a time he struggled to finish a task. He shows Nico ideas. He tells him, "You are doing a good job. I believe you can get it done."

CHAPTER 3

18 CHAPTER 3

Be **mindful** about what others might be going through. Mel is recording a video for drama club, but she is upset about how she did on her math test. Cam shows **compassion**. He says, "I'm sorry about your math test. The video is looking great. I can't wait to see it when it's finished."

WHEN YOU NEED HELP

Sometimes you may be the one struggling. Remind yourself of a time you struggled with something but made it through. Don't be afraid to ask for help.

CHAPTER 3 19

Remember that when you work in a group, you all have the same **goal**. When you all work together, you can accomplish it. Encouraging others helps them feel good and do their best. And you'll feel good, too!

CHAPTER 3

GOALS AND TOOLS

GROW WITH GOALS

Encouraging all members of your group or team can help everyone do their best. How can you encourage others?

Goal: Help motivate the other members of your group. Tell them that you are excited to work with them and that you believe they will all do a great job.

Goal: Point out something specific you like about the work each of your group members is doing.

Goal: If you see someone struggling, ask how you can help. Show empathy. Work together to figure out a way to move forward. Can you help that person start on the next step?

WRITING REFLECTION

Encouraging others and remaining positive are important any time you work with others.

1. Write about a time when working with others went well. How did you and your group members encourage one another?

2. Write about a time someone encouraged you. What did that person say? How did it make you feel?

3. Make a list of encouraging words or phrases. Use these the next time you want to encourage someone.

GLOSSARY

abilities
Skills, or the mental or physical powers to do things.

compassion
A feeling of sympathy for and a desire to help someone who is suffering.

compliment
To make a remark or do something to show admiration or appreciation.

confident
Self-assured and having a strong belief in your own abilities.

constructive feedback
Useful suggestions that contribute to a positive outcome.

empathy
The ability to understand and be sensitive to the thoughts and feelings of others.

encourage
To give someone confidence, usually by using praise and support.

goal
Something you aim to do.

mindful
A mentality achieved by focusing on the present moment and calmly recognizing and accepting your feelings, thoughts, and sensations.

motivate
To encourage someone to do something or want to do something.

patient
Able to put up with problems or delays without getting angry or upset.

positive
Helpful or constructive.

reassure
To make someone feel calm and confident and give the person courage.

rewarding
Offering or bringing satisfaction.

support
To give help, comfort, or encouragement to someone or something.

TO LEARN MORE

Finding more information is as easy as 1, 2, 3.

1. Go to www.factsurfer.com
2. Enter "**encouragingothers**" into the search box.
3. Choose your book to see a list of websites.

INDEX

abilities 7
accomplish 20
ask 5, 14, 19
compassion 19
compliment 9
confident 7
constructive feedback 10
conversations 13
decisions 13
empathy 16
feelings 10
goal 20

help 8, 10, 14, 19, 20
ideas 5, 10, 13, 16
improve 10
listen 14
mindful 19
motivate 8
positive 7, 10
reassure 15
struggle 14, 16, 19
support 7
task 16
upset 19

Blue Owl Books are published by Jump!, 5357 Penn Avenue South, Minneapolis, MN 55419, www.jumplibrary.com

Copyright © 2022 Jump! International copyright reserved in all countries. No part of this book may be reproduced in any form without written permission from the publisher.

Library of Congress Cataloging-in-Publication Data

Names: Colich, Abby, author.
Title: Encouraging others / by Abby Colich.
Description: Minneapolis: Jump!, Inc., 2022. | Series: Working together
Includes index. | Audience: Ages 7–10
Identifiers: LCCN 2021003080 (print)
LCCN 2021003081 (ebook)
ISBN 9781636901176 (hardcover)
ISBN 9781636901183 (paperback)
ISBN 9781636901190 (ebook)
Subjects: LCSH: Encouragement–Juvenile literature. | Helping behavior–Juvenile literature. | Kindness–Juvenile literature.
Classification: LCC BF637.E53 C65 2022 (print)
LCC BF637.E53 (ebook) | DDC 155.4/192–dc23
LC record available at https://lccn.loc.gov/2021003080
LC ebook record available at https://lccn.loc.gov/2021003081

Editor: Eliza Leahy
Designer: Molly Ballanger

Photo Credits: monkeybusinessimages/iStock, cover; Matthias G. Ziegler/Shutterstock, 1; Littlekidmoment/Shutterstock, 3; fstop123/iStock, 4; kali9/iStock, 5, 10–11; FatCamera/iStock, 6–7, 12–13; BGStock72/Shutterstock, 8; vgajic/iStock, 9; mirc3a/Shutterstock, 14; Robert Kneschke/Shutterstock, 15, 20–21; iJeab/Shutterstock, 16–17; LightField Studios/Shutterstock, 18–19.

Printed in the United States of America at Corporate Graphics in North Mankato, Minnesota.

24   GOALS AND TOOLS